SANNA STANLEY

MONKEY SUNDAY

A STORY FROM A CONGOLESE VILLAGE

Frances Foster Books • Farrar, Straus and Giroux • New York

To Bob Blackburn

Copyright © 1998 by Sanna Stanley
Distributed in Canada by Douglas & McIntyre Ltd.
Printed in the United States of America by Worzalla
Designed by Filomena Tuosto
First edition, 1998

Library of Congress Cataloging-in-Publication Data
Stanley, Sanna.
    Monkey Sunday : a story from a Congolese village /
Sanna Stanley. — 1st ed.
        p.   cm.
    Summary: Young Luzolo tries very hard to sit still while
her father preaches at the village Matondo, a celebration
of thanksgiving, but when a puppy, chickens, pigs, goats,
and a monkey show up, it is very difficult.
    ISBN 0-374-35018-3
    [1. Congo (Democratic Republic)—Fiction.   2. Fathers
and daughters—Fiction.   3. Animals—Fiction.]   I. Title.
PZ7.S7895Mo   1998
[E]—DC21   97-18529

"Luzolo, can't you sit still?" her mother asked, tying a knot in Luzolo's hair.

"With an animal nearby?" Her father spoke up. "Impossible."

Luzolo reached for a puppy that plopped down next to her.

"Of course, if you *could* sit still..."

"I know," Luzolo interrupted her father. "Tata Nkondi will say, 'What a good girl the pastor's daughter is.' "

Tata Nkondi had trained Luzolo's father to be the village preacher, and he was coming today to hear Luzolo's father preach.

"Maybe I *can* sit still," said Luzolo.

"Show me," her father dared her.

"Not right now," her mother said. "We can't be late for Matondo."

Luzolo dragged a stick for the puppy to chase and headed up the hill behind her parents to the palm-thatch shelter the village had built for the Matondo.

A Matondo was a celebration of thanksgiving, when people from nearby villages came to visit, bringing gifts of food. It was the first time Luzolo's father had preached at a Matondo, and he wanted everything to go just right.

"Luzolo!" said Tata Nkondi.
"You're growing up."
"I'm even going to sit still today," said Luzolo.
"In that case," said Tata Nkondi, "you can sit with me."
Luzolo waved to her friends and proudly sat next to Tata Nkondi. She dangled her legs, and her toes brushed the puppy's soft, warm fur.
"*Tuyangalala*." Her father started a song. "Sing and celebrate."
"*Tuyangalala, tuyangalalanga*," the people sang back to him.
"We sing and celebrate."

Tin rattles shook. Drums beat. Tata Nkondi clapped and swayed to the music.
A hen and six yellow chicks fluttered about. Luzolo reached down to catch one of the chicks. She felt her father looking at her. "Impossible," he had said. She straightened up, and closed her eyes for the prayer.

"*Kiambote, kieno*," her father shouted. "Hello, everyone."
"*Kiambote,* Pastor," the people shouted back.

Luzolo loved to watch her father preach. He jumped up and down. He shouted. He waved his arms. He yelled at the congregation, and they yelled back at him. Tata Nkondi was the loudest.

A pig squealed. Luzolo peeked behind her. A mama pig with her pink-and-brown piglets made themselves comfortable in a patch of shade.

Two goats tumbled into the shelter. Luzolo reached out her hand, and the goats sniffed her fingers. Her father was smiling. "Impossible," his eyes teased. Tata Nkondi didn't seem to notice. Luzolo clasped her hands in her lap, and the goats scrambled away.

Suddenly, a shriek came from the ceiling. Everyone, even Luzolo's father, looked up.

"*Chiiii-chiiii!*" A monkey was in the rafters, eating a banana! The monkey looked down and carelessly tossed his banana peel. It landed on Tata Nkondi's head.

Luzolo giggled and squirmed. Tata Nkondi shook his finger at the monkey. The monkey shook his finger back at Tata Nkondi. Luzolo's father shook his finger at the congregation, and went right on preaching.

Luzolo's friends reached for the monkey. Luzolo itched to join them, but she stayed in her seat.

"The food!" Luzolo heard her mother cry.

The chickens had pecked a hole in a bag of rice. One of the piglets had climbed into a bowl of fruit. The mama pig wandered by with a mango in her mouth.

"Luzolo, help," her mother called, and lunged for the pig.

"I'm sitting still." Luzolo mouthed the words to her mother.

"Not now," her mother cried, as the pig scrambled away.

"Luzolo, *how* can you sit still?" asked Tata Nkondi, taking the mango from the pig.

The monkey shrieked.

"He wants the mango," Tata Nkondi whispered, handing it to Luzolo.

Luzolo held the mango in her lap. The monkey jumped down from the rafters and begged Luzolo for the mango. Luzolo didn't budge. The monkey climbed up onto the bench and into her arms.

"Luzolo!" her mother called again.

Then the monkey grabbed the mango and stuffed it in his mouth. He squeezed out of Luzolo's arms.

Luzolo looked up at her father. "Impossible," she agreed, and shrugged her shoulders. Her father was laughing.

The children shouted. The hen clucked, the pigs squealed, the goats bleated, and the puppy barked. Tin rattles shook. Drums beat.

"*Vaneno, luvaneno, vaneno.*" The offering song started. "Bring your gifts."

"*Lu batata, vana mu kitata,*" the people sang, while the men danced up to the front with their offerings. "Come, men, bring your gifts."

"*Lu bamama, vana mu kimama,*" the people sang. "Come, women, bring your gifts." The women danced up to the offering basket and back to their benches, while the children rounded up the animals.

Out went the pig, the two pink-and-brown piglets, the six yellow chicks, the hen, the goats, and the puppy.

"*Lu bamwana, vana mu kimwana*," the people sang. "Come, children, bring your gifts."

Now it was the children's turn. Luzolo and her friends skipped to the front of the church to put their offerings in the basket.

Her father's face stretched in a big grin. "It's not every Sunday a monkey comes to visit," he said.

"Watch me *now*," Luzolo said.

She danced back to her bench.
While Tata Nkondi said the
final prayer, Luzolo sat very,
very still.

But not for long.

AUTHOR'S NOTE

Monkey Sunday is set in the western region of the Democratic Republic of Congo, where I spent eight years of my childhood. It is a large country, with many different languages. The people where I lived spoke Kikongo.

"Matondo" is a Kikongo word which means "celebration of thanksgiving." People from surrounding villages come together for three or four days of singing, dancing, preaching, and feasting. The villagers bring gifts to each other and to the local church. These gifts are anything one has to give— from coins to eggs, fruit and vegetables, chickens, and goats.

Tata Nkondi was a famous teacher and preacher in our region. He loved any celebration, and was often the guest speaker at a Matondo.

As is the custom for any large service or meeting, a thatch shelter is built by the host village. Since the shelter has only a roof and is not closed in by walls or windows and doors, it is common for village animals to wander in.

Though monkeys usually stay in the jungle or forested areas, once, when my family and I were visiting a church, there was a great commotion in the rafters. Everyone looked up, and there was a monkey eating a banana. This was the first monkey Sunday. My new *Monkey Sunday* takes place at the opening service of a Matondo.